Whatever Happens

(English Poems)

T. Jeong

Contents

1. Whatever Happens

I don't mind whatever happens to me
Even though it is serious or not
Everything would stay for a while
And then those pass away
I would like not to resist those come to me
And not to be obsessed with those go away
I will stand by myself whatever happens to me
I will just look over everything with empty
heart

2. To the west

I left blindly along the west road

Because there is a mountain, I meet the mountain
Because there is water, I meet water
I meet a person because there is a person

I don't know where it is
I don't know if I'm going right
I just went out to the west

All the relationships I meet and bump into
I spilled it by passing

Without even thinking about why I should go
Without a clear purpose
I went endlessly toward the west

There was nothing special at the west end

With the blue sea spreading before my eyes

The red sunset dyed the sky
It was the all at the end of the road

I sat on the beach and looked at the western sky

'Cause I can't go any further
'Cause my limit is here
I sent my heart to the sky

I become a heartless person
I felt free at the end of the world

3. Where are you

I went out to sea
I wanted to hear that sound

I saw only the horizon in the distance
with the waves breaking

I've climbed the mountain
I wanted to find at least a trace

I only saw the peaks shrouded in mist
without the echo returning

4. Wind and heart

I put my heart on the wind

I don't know where to go
Leaving everything as it is
I just put it on the wind

Because I can't go
Because I can't even go

Even with the help of the wind
I wished to get there

Even if the wind doesn't know where it is
Even if the wind doesn't reach there

Just put your heart on it
There was nothing I could do

I saw the wind go
Standing absent-mindedly

I just looked endlessly that the wind goes

5. I feel sorry

Haven't bloomed in a long time
Looking only at the future in the shadow of darkness
I feel bad for it

Pain of the past
Waiting for the sunlight in the sadness and loneliness
I feel bad for it

Still bound by the wounds of the past
Living hard today without free mind
I feel bad for it

6. Where are you going

In this deep night
I walked alone without anyone
Where should I go

The sound of a stream flowing with melting snow
Even though it flows so powerfully,
Where am I going

Those white clouds flowing with the wind
You can go anywhere as you like
Where can I go

7. Fate

Beyond eons of time
passing through infinite space
Not a planned space
It's not what I wanted

Probability that cannot happen
A nearly impossible event

Here
This place
Now

By existing like that

Now into the world of the heart
With the undeniable wings of the soul

Able to see the world
With that fate

8. You

You waited silently
I see the sky in your heart

You watched in silence
I see the stars in your heart

The wind blew
My heart flew too

I flap my wings towards you
Flying through the blue sky

Freely
Comfortably

Even in the dark
Following the starlight

Towards you
Flew like that

9. At the edge of a cliff

Stood on the edge of a high cliff
There isn't even a steep downhill

I saw the sky and clouds
I can't fly with wings

The wind brushed my face
I can't catch it with my own strength

I dreamed of falling
There is no choice but to be infinitely free

10. Train sound

I can hear the train
It's time to leave
I bury my heart like that

I see a red sunset
The hot midday sun
Now I'm biting it

White clouds flow by
I don't know where
To that distant place

11. Next to me

Even if you aren't pretty
Even if you don't know much
Even if there are many things lacking

I hope you are by my side

Even if messy
Even if not mature
Even if stubborn

I hope you are by my side

Even if we fight with each other
Even if we fight and get upset

I hope you are by my side

12. Even if it's misaligned

There are things that go wrong in life
There is bound to be

I'm trying to make it right
I don't think that's necessary

If you know my sincerity
Everything will be understood.

Life is just as you want it to be
I don't think it would be

Even if something is out of sync
I just want to live with it

Life is amazing
It's not that big of a deal
I think I know now

13. Beyond the rainbow

Somewhere beyond the rainbow
There will be that person

Across the distant blue sea
There will be that person

A place I can't go to
There will be that person

When will it be?
Where is it?

A place where heart and mind touch
That person will be there

14. Tear

They say it's okay
But I know it's not okay

They say it's not hard
But I know it's hard

Although you smile at me
But I know you’re crying inside

They say it doesn't hurt
But I know it hurts a lot

You say you don't need much
But I know a lot is needed

You say we're there
But there is still a long way to go

When will those tears stop
I really don't know

15. Candlelight

Burning myself endlessly
Melting and flowing
Without hesitation
I spent time like that

Without expecting anything
All you have to do is giving yourself
I thought it was everything

Time passes
Now there's more to burn
There was nothing left
We're coming to the end

And then
without any trace
I guess I should leave

The light that has been shining, albeit weakly,
Does anyone even remember?

16. Holding hands

Even though I had nothing, he held my hands
Even if I didn't know anything, he recognized me

Even though I was different, he accepted me
Even if there was a mistake, there was no problem

We turned our heads and shed tears
We looked at each other and laughed and laughed

It was a blessing to walk together
We was happy to see the same sky

17. Mom's nagging

Mom said to me again today

It's cold so dress warmly
Be careful because the road is slippery
Don't skip meals
Visit to the hospital
Don't be too late
Take it easy and work hard

Even though you know how old I am
I guess she still consider me like a kid

Mom's nagging is now
It doesn't sound like nagging

I hope it lasts forever

18. Shall we meet as stars?

In dark night sky
Shall we meet as stars?

Newly blooming in spring
Shall we meet as flowers?

Flying in the sky
Shall we meet as birds?

Forgetting all that
Shall we meet again when we are reborn?

Longing becomes resentment
It's buried in my heart

19. I will go back

I will go back now
To a warm and comfortable place

I will go back now
To a place of rest and comfort

I will go back now
To the place that welcomes me with a smile

I will go back now
To the place where I originally was

20. Existence

Having is not greed
I don't even wish for it

Being is not far away
It's not something you can't do.

Existence is not vain
It's not suffering

Where I am is important
The person next to me is everything
That's why I exist

Being there is a pleasure
It's now

Today I am
That's why I feel it
I feel alive
It is the existence

21. Nothingness

Nothingness is
It's enlightenment

From me
There shouldn't be

From thoughts
You must be free

This way or that way
It's not biased

I'm not obsessed
does not claim

Escape from pain
doesn't act

See what you see
I accept it as is

Because there is nothing
everything disappears

That is the nothingness

22. Becoming

Becoming
It's a change
It's awake

Not by itself
You have to do it yourself

Although I'm alone
I'm not lonely
I have to go far
It should last a long time

Also
not oriented
Doesn't hit
It flows naturally

Unintentional
Put it down
I just leave it to you.

So it's comfortable
I am satisfied
There is no end
It can't come true

That is the Becoming

23. Here I am

I came from a world of nothing
We must go to the world of nothing

My presence is also for the sake of my absence
It's not about heading towards nothing

My wish is for existence
It's for my daily life too

My existence is for the purpose of being me
I'm trying to become a better me

My first time may be meaningless and nothing
My later is meaningless

That's why I'm here now

24. Hope it continues

May the days of hope continue
Despair lasts only for a moment

May the days of joy continue
Sadness only lasts for a moment

May the days of happiness continue
Misfortune lasts only for a moment

May the days of joy continue
The pain only stays for a moment

May the days of love continue
Hatred only lasts for a moment

May the bright days continue
The darkness stays for a while

Even if this is a dream
I hope it continues like that

25. Morning star

The time we spent together is gone
Memories are fading now

My warm heart also disappears
There is no longer any longing left

Everything disappears like that
What should I do with my empty heart

Deep night, no sleep comes
Only the morning star is shining

26. Vacant land

In the empty space of my soul
There is only a desolate feeling of silence

That nothing
Without being able to stay
Time was just piling up

Like a desert sand dune
It was a dry empty land

Now on my own
I will fill the place and replace it.

The warm sunlight stays
With a moist drizzle falling
Beautiful sunset and
Birds chirping
To a beautiful place

So rich and a free place

I will make it myself

27. The road

I walked in search of the path of life
Without knowing where it is
I walked that path alone

In the hazy fog
With a light on in my heart
I'm tired from walking alone

On that endless road
share your heart
There was no one

How long is the road left
Will I be able to walk until the end
The silence on the road makes my heart flutter

28. Crying bird

Cry, cry, bird
It's sad, so cry, bird

Enjoy as much as you deserve
I stayed long enough

I have too many regrets
I have too many regrets

Now I have to leave
I have to leave this place

Cry, cry, bird
It's sad, so cry, bird

29. Everyone goes away

In the place where everyone has gone
there was no one

Walking around alone
I just stare blankly

The wind blowing from somewhere
It only makes dust fly

The sun sets over west mountains
darkness is coming

Staying there alone
I raise my head and look at the distant sky

Today it is full of clouds
Not a single star shines

30. Even if feel sad

Even if I'm sad, I'm not so sad
Because I know it's fate

Even though I miss you, I don't miss you much
Because I know I can't help it

Even if I hate you, I don't hate you
Because I know it can be done

Even though it hurts, it doesn't hurt a lot
Because I know it can't be healed

Now I look at the blue sky
I send my heart to the clouds

Now I look at the stars in the night sky
I bury my heart in the sky

31. I can't see it

Even if I look back, I can't see it
No matter how much I search, I can't find it

It looks like it's coming running from somewhere at any moment.
No matter how long I wait, there is no news

Did I live in a dream?
Am I dreaming now?

Cutting through the empty space of my heart
It seems like time is not on my side

It's nowhere now
My heart seems to have disappeared

32. Ladder of hope

To look far away
I won't do it

Here
Somewhere nearby
I would like to hope

That's enough for me
There's nothing more to wish for
Now I know for sure

Even a little joy
Even small happiness

If only that were given
I think of it as a ladder of hope

33. The petals are falling

Like flower petals falling and blowing in the wind
I don't know when and where I'll go

Like the brilliant dew disappearing in the sunlight
There is no guarantee of remaining time

Is it not enough to survive today?
There is nothing to hope for in being alive

I have a lot of regrets about things I couldn't achieve,
but I am satisfied with what I was able to do

I feel a lot of shame because of my shortcomings
It will be enough to keep it as a beautiful memory

Because I was here
Because I felt many things
Because I have had enough experience
Even if it falls like a flower petal, there will be no regrets

34. I hope you don't get sick

It's okay if I suffer for you
I hope you don't have a hard time

It's okay for me to be unhappy instead
I hope you are happy

It's okay if I suffer for you
I hope you rest in peace

It's okay if I get criticized instead.
I hope you don't get criticized

Because I can hurt you instead
I hope you don't get sick

What I can do for you
I really wish there were more

35. Cause it disappears

Could always disappear
Because they are things

At what moment will it disappear?
Because I don't know

No need to think that anything is mine

I can't have anything
There is no need to feel sorry

Something to consider precious
Something to consider meaningful
Because someday it will disappear

Just holding in your heart
I just take it out sometimes

36. You are not alone

The blazing sun shines down
Even when crossing the middle of the desert
I wasn't alone

That distant horizon
Even when passing through an endless continent
I wasn't alone

I can't see the black clouds in front of me
Even when going through a storm
I wasn't alone

The endless snowfall and
Even when passing through the shivering cold
I wasn't alone

Because I wasn't alone
I am here now

37. Before spring ends

Although the dazzling spring days are in full swing
but someone maybe not

There are beautiful flowers everywhere,
but someone can't even see a single flower

Whether you feel spring
Whether you feel it or not
Spring is slowly passing by

It won't come back
Spring is going like this

Where do I stand

Enjoy this spring to the fullest
Are you looking forward to another season?

I didn't even know this spring had come
Are you even afraid of the coming summer?

Before this spring passes
Shouldn't I spread my arms out?

Toward that dazzling sky
Shouldn't I raise my head?

Today too, somewhere in this spring
A flower that once bloomed is fading

Before another flower fades tomorrow
Shouldn't I look at that flower?

38. Tears at night

A place that can't be reached
Maybe it's the pain itself

That there is nothing to wish for
It may not be able to feel alive

Existence is like that
With pain and resignation
It seems to be filling up

Maybe things like that
make the world beautiful

In this deepening night
Another I inside myself shed tears

39. I wanted to ask to fate

I have no choice but to walk that path

Because there was no choice
Because it has reached its limit

There is no other road besides that road

At least that's the way
I was able to live because I had

Even if the same situation comes
The choice will remain the same

But to fate
I wanted to ask
Why did you do that to me?
Why was that only way given?

40. It seems like it has passed

It seems like it has passed by
I can't believe it
It seems like it passed like that

It seems like it has flown by
irreversibly
It seems like it went by like that

I don't think I can catch it
Even if I gesture
I probably won't be able to catch it

41. That look

That familiar look
forever
will not be forgotten

A familiar voice
forever
will remain

The most precious
The sight and voice
Because it was my beginning and my end

In this land
Until life ends
It will stay in your heart

42. Two hearts

Maybe I had two hearts
One has already stopped
Looks like the other one is running

Maybe I had two hearts
One heart has already disappeared
I guess I live with the rest of my heart

Maybe I had two souls
One soul is gone
I guess I live with the rest of my soul

43. Unknown

In the arms of an angel
It's like I'm trying to go to an unknown place

Sunlight shines
Passing by a bright place

With the starlight as my friend
Without fear even in dark places

Not coming back
Beyond the moment of time

Lost feelings
Crossing the world of transcendence

With the scent of flowers
With the wings of a butterfly

44. A little thing

It may look unsightly
It won't even be noticeable
Everyone passes by
It doesn't show up even if it's not there
No one close to it even knows

No need to be disappointed
Don't even be upset
There is no reason to be sad

It's just not the time yet

At that place
take root deeper
little by little
Just absorb water and nutrients

Time has passed

People who didn't recognize even ignore you

Now
under you
to avoid sunlight
to avoid the rain
They're resting comfortably

You are to spread many branches
to become a big tree
and the source of life

You were a precious seed

45. Entanglement

Because this was there, that is there
Because that exists, this exists.

If it weren't for this, there wouldn't be anything
Without that, there would be no this.

That person is hurting because of me
Because that person is hurting, others are hurting too

That person is happy because of me
Because that person is happy, others are happy too

That makes me happy
Because of me, others are happy too

Maybe life is all about entanglement
Entanglement creates another entanglement

46. Separated and together

If we can do even a little bit together
Even if your feelings are a little different
Even if the beginning and end do not match

Separately and together
Don't hurt your heart
For a long time

47. Burying the years

Because I went too far
I couldn't come back

I will go that far
I didn't even think about it

In a place that is not my place
That there should be
I didn't know it would be this hard

Even if I try to come back now
I can't come back

Forever there
I just miss this place

Now like that
I'm trying to bury the years

48. Son's back

I looked at your back endlessly

There were many people
I only saw you

With your past
your presence and
your future
I was watching it from the spot

I hope you do well

I was stuck in that place
I looked your back endlessly

49. One star

In the dark night sky
A star appeared from somewhere

Those anxious years
Because I was afraid of disappearing forever

Not a short time
The night sky I looked at endlessly

Forever in that place
Not disappearing
Become the North Star

50. Winter in the mountains

In the middle of winter

Walking along a desolate mountain path
I fastened my collar

At the mountain temple I found alone
silence flows

In the fading sunlight
The sunset is distant

Tree branches swaying in the wind
The sound of wind chime heard

With the sound of birds diligently finding their home
Quiet peace comes

It's cold but I hope it's not cold
It's hard but I hope it's not hard
It maybe my greed

In this deep mountain
All that futility
I'm going to put it down

51. White solitude

An unknown sadness
Being pushed into my chest

In secret loneliness
My heart is empty

The inevitable fate
frustrates me

On the other side of a miserable life
It's just frustrating

My loneliness is like that
piled up and piled up
With the passing time
It turned white

52. Just love

I can love because I am worthy of love,
but maybe just love

Because existence is so perfect
its mere existence is enough

Just to love
my existence
I'm trying to make it big

Hurting me
Even if I make you cry
By embracing everything
I just want to love you

53. Farewell to memories

Memories of the distant beyond
Now we must say goodbye

It may be a beautiful memory
but it has no meaning anymore

Although I may think of it sometimes
It just hurts my heart

Now to make new memories
I retrace my steps

What lies ahead
I don't know if there will be
I will move on as I always do

54. I see it

Looking at it at the end of life
everything is like smoke
It's disappearing

Hoping for it in despair
It's still precious time
I hope it stays

I hope for it in patience
Now at the end
I hope I can reach you

I wish for it in pain
Deep wounds may be healed quickly

55. Evening bells

Far western sky
The sunset is colored

A chilling wind
The clouds are moving away

Deepening darkness
The earth is asleep

Somewhere quietly
I hear the evening bells

That sound comes inside me
With a heavy heart
Peace is coming

56. Wind chimes

In the west mountains
The red sun
It goes by day by day

The valley
The clear water
It flows without stopping

Somewhere
In the sound of the wind chimes

My wandering heart
find the way

57. Like a star

Far away, beyond the distant mountains
I don't know if there was

I can't even hear it
In a place that couldn't be seen
Maybe he was hiding

Are you trying to answer my cries?
Are you trying to wipe away my tears?

Like the stars in the sky
It may have appeared in the dark of night

I hope it's not a passing star
my heart was praying for it

58. Following the water

It has to flow with the water
I guess I did it

It has to flow with the wind
I guess I did it

The higher the mountain, the higher it is
If the river is deep, it is as deep as it is
I guess it had to go that way

I wonder if I can still feel that way now

As soon as it rains
As soon as it snows

I guess I should go that way

59. Beyond the blue

There was something beyond the blue. I wanted to go there beyond the blue. Something was holding it back, preventing it from going over. Something beyond the blue looked this way. They stood in silence, recognizing each other. An unknown string approached. I wanted to be tied to that string. I hoped to follow that string and cross the border. I wanted to leave this place. I knew I had to let go of everything. Suddenly the wind blew. I could have predicted that the wind would blow. Everything has disappeared. I missed the blue that would never come back. I don't even know where Blue is anymore. I couldn't reach beyond the blue from the beginning. Now, only the blue in my heart remains.

60. Rain of fate

The mountain was high. Why is there a mountain that I want to climb but can't? The mountain is calling me. Why is the mountain standing there that I can't get to even if I want to? I looked at the mountain. The mountain does not know the weight of the fate that can only be seen. You are not the master and I am not the master. Even if you think you are free because you are not the owner, you are not free. I could see the road. I could see the road leading to the mountain. But he didn't come forward. I knew that I had no confidence in going down that path, and that path had no meaning. Rainwater soaked my face. It flowed from above my head. Even though my whole body was wet, there was nothing I could do. It was decided that all the rain would catch. The inevitable rain of fate fell like that. Now I'm leaving with my destiny. I leave with my back to the mountain, listening to the sound of rain.

61. Why did the white come?

I didn't know where the white would go. Since there was no way, I thought I would stay. Before I knew it, a path appeared and I set off along it. I thought it would be there for a long time. I didn't know time passed and I didn't know things were changing. Not knowing whether to leave, I just looked at the white. I don't know when it will come. I just watched it go by because it might never come again. I couldn't figure out what they were saying. It seemed like he was looking back, and he seemed to be talking. I didn't know why I came and disappeared like that. If you're only staying for a while, don't come. Don't wait for white. Knowing that I would leave and that I would not be able to come back, I waved my hand like that and put it in my heart.

62. Yellow

It's a borderline. A life that seems to be cut off continues, and the dying candle is still burning. I asked whether it was impossible for this place and that place to be different, and whether there could be no boundaries. Someone answered. Everything is one and there are no boundaries. What you see isn't everything. It is invisible to my eyes. It seemed like what he said wasn't true. I cut off my yellow tail. I wondered if it would grow a tail again. I cut myself off, even though I knew the scars I caused would last forever. The tail did not regenerate. I didn't have those genes. My heart is getting colder and it doesn't warm up. Memories that disappear do not come back. The feeling of dislike doesn't get better. For me, only boundaries exist and I can't do anything about them. The yellow has faded. To the point of being invisible. Still, there was a boundary for me.

63. The valley

The valley was deep. So scary to go down. I didn't hesitate to take a step because I thought I might not be able to come back up after going down. But there was no other way. I couldn't figure out why this deep valley was in front of me. There was no other choice. There was no other way than to go down into that deep valley. It was only then that I realized that going down was harder than going up. There was nothing to see on the way down. I don't yet know where the end of the valley will be, but the sun shining overhead tells me that I will reach the bottom someday and be able to get out of the valley and go up to it again.

64. The voice

You don't call me. When I stand in hazy fog, I can't hear the sound of waiting. I don't know how long I can stay. I don't know if the time to leave may suddenly come. I don't know how long I can wait, but I can't hear it yet. I don't know when my fate of waiting will end. I can't tell whether my wanting to lose. The sound will only be heard without you, since you are the main character of the sound, waiting for that sound may inevitably become a torture of hope. The night is getting deeper, but my heart, waiting for that sound, cannot know the depth of this night.

65. Wind

I left myself to the drifting wind. I didn't know where I would end up, but I wanted to believe in the invisible wind. Whether it flows over the mountains, into the sea, to a warm place or to a cold place, it is not that important. Having a place I can go comforts me in the loneliness of my existence, and being able to leave it to the wind brings peace to my small life, so it doesn't matter where I wander. Now I become the wind, and the wind becomes me, and no matter what obstacles there are, I can overcome them, so I no longer struggle with my strength. I see stars on the wind, I see the sun on the wind, and no matter where I go in this world, I meet my inner self there.

66. Space

It was not that nothing existed in the empty space. Since a being that can fill the space is possible, the existence of the space itself opens up the possibility of a certain being. Because that space was nothing, it could become anything. The existence of space itself had to have meaning. Therefore, emptiness is no different from being completely filled. I am willing to abandon myself because I am confident that I can find my true self through that abandonment. What is important is not what I look like, but what is important is my empty self, so I boldly let go of everything I have taken up until now and throw it away without any regrets. I find my whole self in my empty self.

67. After your leaving

You shouldn't have left like that. Without even knowing it, with your own thoughts, you willingly left the path of no return. I just feel sorry for not being able to catch you because I don't know what's on the road. You may be able to get through it on your own, but you may get tired of the obstacles you face and lose a lot of your life. My confidence in myself may have made me take that path, but it may have been due to a momentary misunderstanding, so I can only look at you from far and am only reminiscing about the time I spent with you. Not having anything to do is a different matter from love, so I just hope that you can bear the weight of life that the world will give you. Someday you will remember me for not letting you leave. But when that time comes, I might be looking at you from that blue star.

68. The road

I set off on my way without knowing where to go. It was not courage, much less fate. I set out on the road, pushed by some unknown force. I didn't know which way to go or how far to go. I may have been convinced in my heart, but I left because I believed there was something better. I couldn't tell if I was going the right way or the wrong way. I knew it was a long road, but I never thought I would get help from anyone. Of course I thought I had to go alone, but I still wanted to have a friend to talk to. But that was just my small wish. Now I feel like I can find out what will be at the end of this road without having to go there. But I also know that I cannot stop, so I am willing to walk this path again today.

69. Snow mountain

I climbed a white snow-covered mountain. I moved forward through the snow. I had no choice but to move forward like that, forgetting about the cold and not knowing how difficult it was. I felt like I had lost something and thought it was in the quiet snow-covered mountains. I wandered all over the mountain, but couldn't find anything. I couldn't come down from that mountain. Because there is nowhere else to look. Something precious ended like that.

70. Green star

It seems that no one lived on the green star. Even the stretched sound waves spread out and disappeared, leaving no resonance whatsoever, leaving silence all around. If it wasn't a vacuum, I couldn't even tell if there was a medium, so I couldn't find any traces. Why was I expecting something here? Why did I find it in this unlikely place? Wouldn't it have been better to wander in a desolate desert or a vast ocean? I don't know why, but was I convinced that some nature led me here? Was it because he wanted to confirm the impossibility even though he knew it was impossible? Why can't I resist the temptation to shout in this place where I can't even hear the echo? I just want to see you walking silently towards the western sky, where even the green color is now turning red, and someday you will get on a horse and run while blowing dust.

Whatever happens

초판 발행 2024년 1월 25일

지은이 정태성
펴낸이 도서출판 코스모스
펴낸곳 도서출판 코스모스
주소 충북 청주시 서원구 신율로 13
전화 043-231-7027
팩스 050-4374-5501

ISBN 979-11-91926-71-2

값 10,000원